Collecting DARKNESS

A Fable for All Ages

Story & Illustration by
SARAH DETWEILER FARRUGIA

ISBN 978-0-5784-7128-0

Dedicated to my Mia,
who shines so brightly
that it is hard to see
the Darkness.

In a village no different from yours or mine...

...there lived a woman who collected Darkness.

The Others in her village
thought her to be very odd.

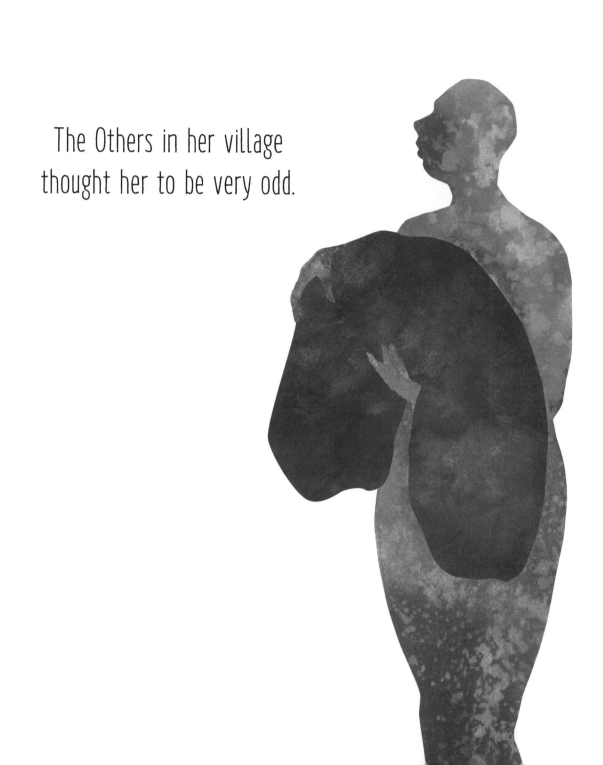

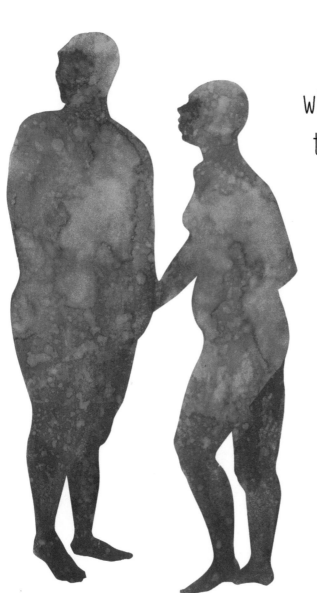

Why would anyone
collect Darkness
when they just wanted
to give theirs away?

BUT SHE COLLECTED
DARKNESS ANYWAY.

The Darkness was not difficult for her to find.

At times, she wouldn't even be looking for it,
and it would just appear.

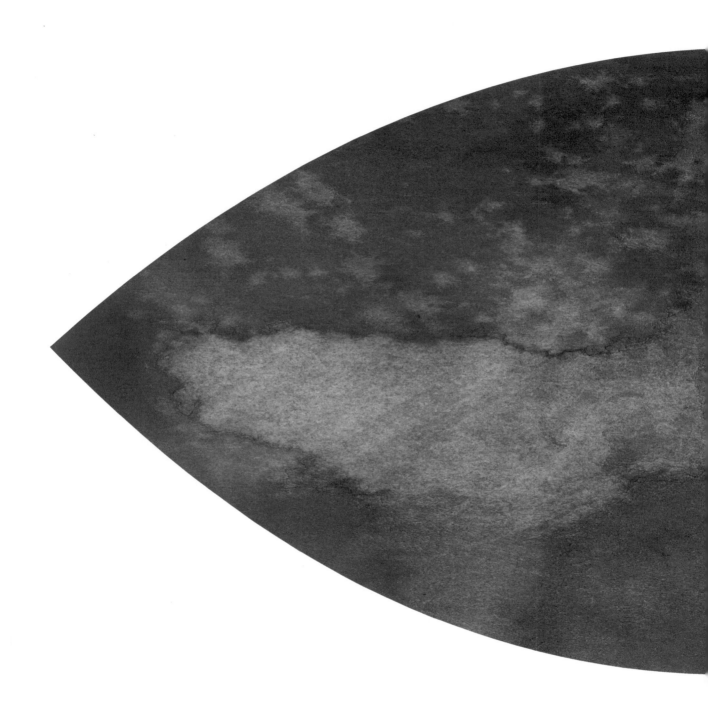

If she closed her eyes,
she could see it everywhere.

There were times when the Darkness
took her right to the edge.

And other times
she found herself
deep in a hole.

When she passed an Other with Darkness,
she would carry it away for them.

Sometimes, the Darkness felt like her only friend.

On occasion,
she would come across
a moment so breathtaking
that she would have to
pause to take a look.

But the Darkness always
found its way back
into her thoughts.

And when the woman who collected Darkness
could carry no more, she gathered it all together...

...and released it into the sky.

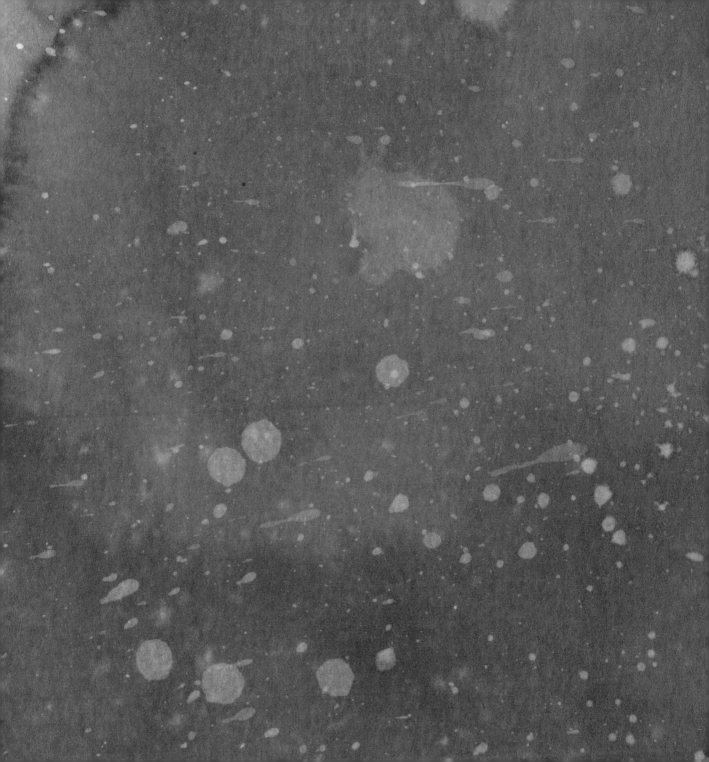

Standing beneath the most incredible, star-filled sky,
the Others finally understood...

...that sometimes without Darkness,
it is hard to see *the light.*

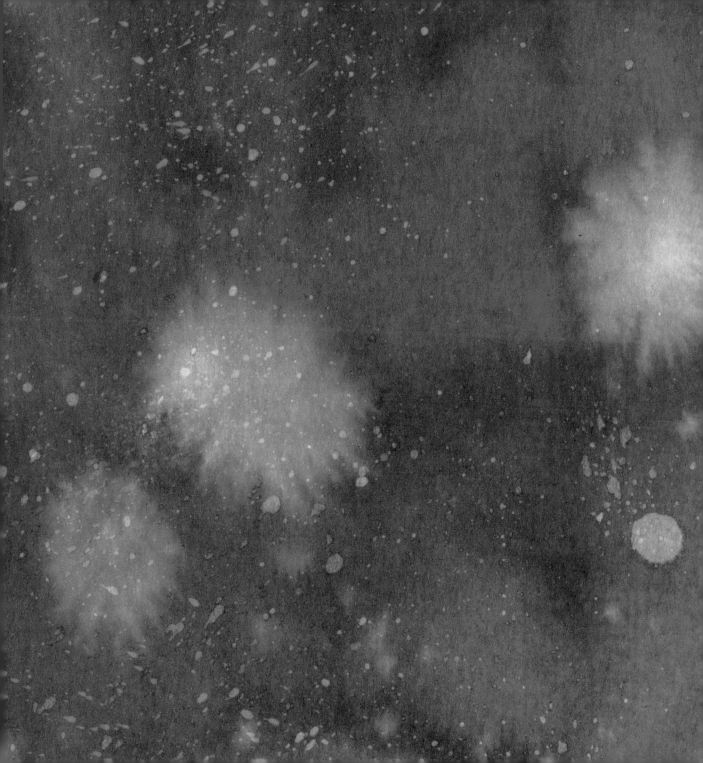

This illustrated fable for all ages began with a single illustration by author and illustrator, Sarah Detweiler Farrugia. The story developed slowly over time, each night as she nursed her daughter to sleep.

In the Darkness, this story found life.

CPSIA information can be obtained
at www.ICGtesting.com
Printed in the USA
LVHW071744281019
635572LV00004B/10/P

9780578471280